The Barn Owls

Tony Johnston

Illustrated by
Deborah Kogan Ray

TALEWINDS

A Charlesbridge Imprint

For Lynn and Michael Donovan
—T.J.

To Karen and Nicole
—D.K.R.

The barn has stood
in the wheat field
one hundred years
at least.

Owls have slept there
all day long
and dozed in the scent
of wheat.

Sometimes by day
an owl awakes
to a shadow
—or nothing
at all—
and leaves the barn
through a bale
of light

and glides to the top
of an oak
and calls.

Sometimes nothing
answers.

Sometimes something
does.

Sometimes by day an owl
goes floating
away, away

to where wheat and sky
are one.

Then it floats back
to the barn.

By night
one by one stars
come out
and blink.

One by one owls
wake up
and blink

and hunt for mice
while moons swell
and shrink.

Owls have hunted
in this place,

mice have hidden
in this wheat
one hundred years
at least.

Where owls hunted,
spiders spun
to hold the barn
to earth.

Where owls hunted,
long snakes sunned
and split their skins
like chaff
and left.

And bees hummed
their hymn
of wheat.

Eggs have hatched
in the loft of the barn
one by one
white and warm.

Old owls watching,
new owls born
in the redwood barn
in the whisper of wheat,

to grow up
and sleep
and wake
and blink

and hunt for mice
as they always have.

One hundred years
at least.

Published by Charlesbridge Publishing
85 Main Street, Watertown, MA 02472
(617) 926-0329
www.charlesbridge.com

Library of Congress Cataloging-in-Publication Data
Johnston, Tony, date.
The barn owls/Tony Johnston; illustrated by Deborah
Kogan Ray.
        p. cm.
"A Talewinds book."
Summary: For at least one hundred years, generations
of barn owls have slept, hunted, called, raised their
young, and glided silently above the wheat fields around
an old barn.
        ISBN 0-88106-981-7 (reinforced for library use)
        ISBN 0-88106-982-5 (softcover)
1. Barn owl—Juvenile fiction. [1. Barn owl—Fiction.
2. Owls—Fiction.] I. Ray, Deborah Kogan, 1940-
ill. II Title.
PZ10.3.J715Bar 2000
[E]—dc21   99-18763

Printed in the United States of America
(hc) 10 9 8 7 6 5 4 3
(sc) 10 9 8 7 6 5 4 3 2

The illustrations in the book were done in transparent
watercolor and watercolor pencil on 140lb. Arches Hot
Press paper.
The display type and text type were set in Top Hat.
Color separations were made by Eastern Rainbow,
Derry, New Hampshire.
Printed and bound by Worzalla Publishing Company,
Stevens Point, Wisconsin
Production supervision by Brian G. Walker
Designed by Diane M. Earley
This book was printed on recycled paper.